For Tilly — J.W.

For Amelie, Arlo, Magali, Phoebe, Sam and Tom — A.R.

Also by Jeanne Willis and Adrian Reynolds:

I'M SURE I SAW A DINOSAUR

MINE'S BIGGER THAN YOURS!

THAT'S NOT FUNNY!

WHO'S IN THE LOO?

First published in Great Britain in 2013 by Andersen Press Ltd.,
20 Vauxhall Bridge Road, London SW1V 2SA.
Published in Australia by Random House Australia Pty.,
Level 3, 100 Pacific Highway, North Sydney, NSW 2060.
Text copyright © Jeanne Willis, 2013.
Illustration copyright © Adrian Reynolds, 2013.
The rights of Jeanne Willis and Adrian Reynolds to be identified as
the author and illustrator of this work have been asserted by them in
accordance with the Copyright, Designs and Patents Act, 1988.
All rights reserved.
Colour separated in Switzerland by Photolitho AG, Zürich.
Printed and bound in Malaysia by Tien Wah Press.
Adrian Reynolds has used watercolours in this book.

10   9   8   7   6   5   4   3   2   1

British Library Cataloguing in Publication Data available.
ISBN 978 1 84939 533 5

UPSIDE DOWN BABIES

JEANNE WILLIS
ADRIAN REYNOLDS

ANDERSEN PRESS

Once when the world tipped upside down.

The earth went blue and the sky went brown.

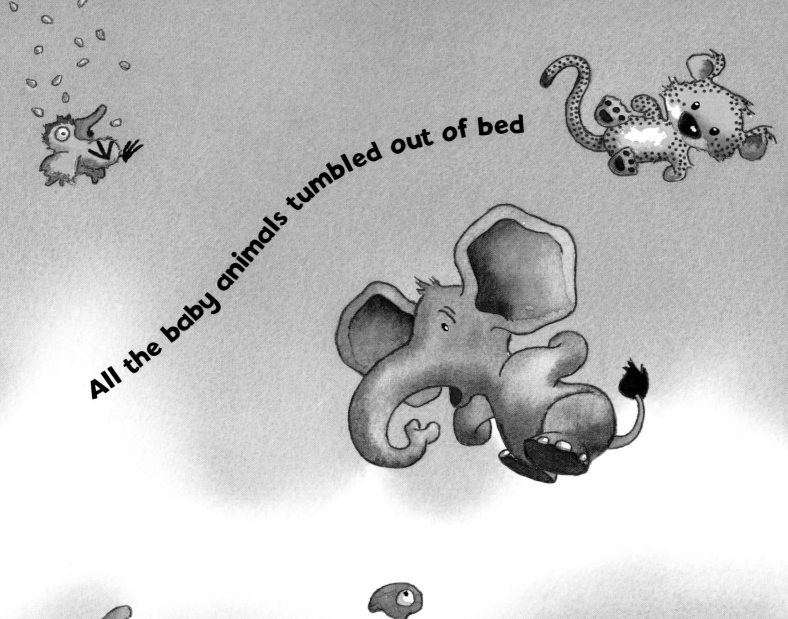

All the baby animals tumbled out of bed

And ended up
with very funny mums instead.

Piglet went **ker-plonk** in a parrot's nest.

Porky and pink with no feathers on his chest.

"What a funny baby, no matter how I try,"
Mummy Parrot said, "this chick won't fly!"

Tortoise

made a

splash!

in a big blue lake,

Shelly and scaly and bald as a snake.

"Whatever shall I do with a kid like him?"
Mummy Otter said. "This pup won't swim!"

Lion Cub fell in a field on his head,
"Eat up your grass, dear," Mummy Cow said.

The cub got cross and stamped his feet,
"I'm a carnivore!" he roared.

Baby Bunny

bounced

into Squirrel's drey,

He clung

to a branch

with his claws

all day.

He couldn't climb up

or down or round.

He was born in

a rabbit hole

underground.

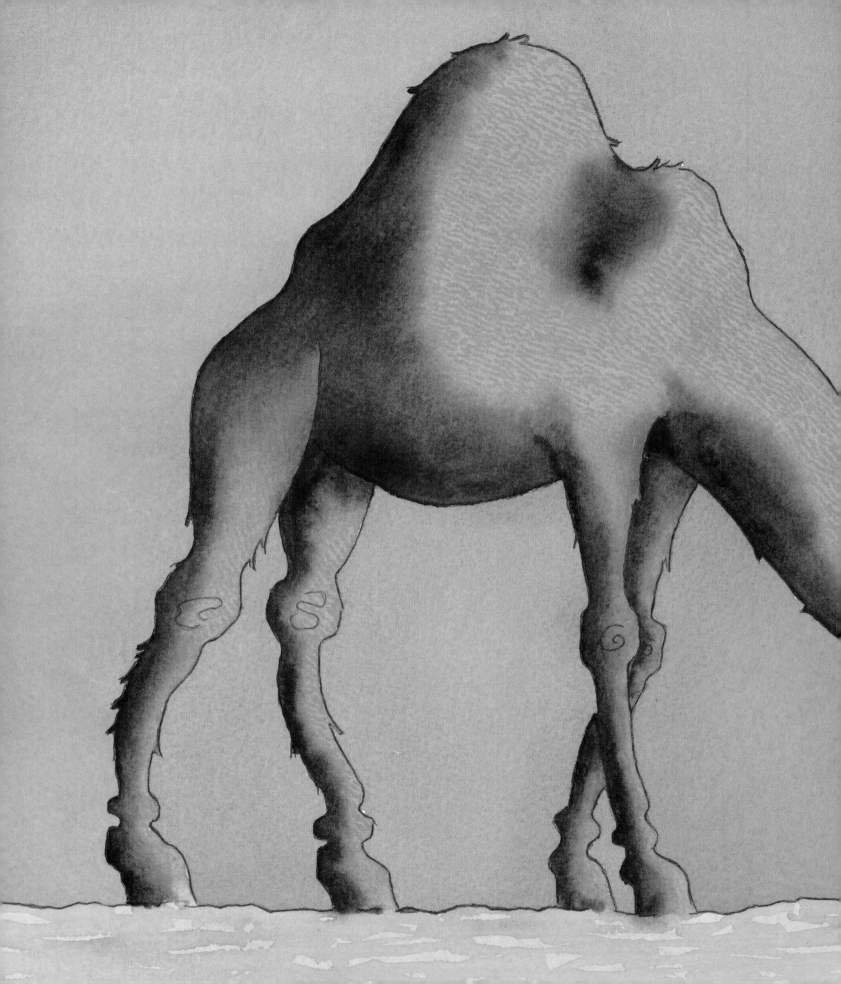

Polar Bear landed in the desert sand.
Poor Mummy Camel couldn't understand
Why he had the hump and growled a lot.
There wasn't any snow. He was far too hot!

Baby Rooster flopped into Mummy Owl's tree,
He woke her at dawn crowing "Cock-a-doodle-dee!"

Owls sleep all morning but roosters like to play,
"Wake up!" he cried. "It's the cock-a-doodle-day!"

As for Baby Elephant and Mummy Kangaroo,
He couldn't do the kind of things a joey likes to do.

He tried to ride inside her pouch
but he was such a lump.

"Hop along!" she said to him, but elephants can't jump.

**Mrs Cheetah felt that Baby Sloth was rather slow,
A metre every morning was as fast as he could go.**

Mrs Sloth found Baby Cheetah really far too fast,
He ran rings around her and was always racing past.

Then the world went downside-up

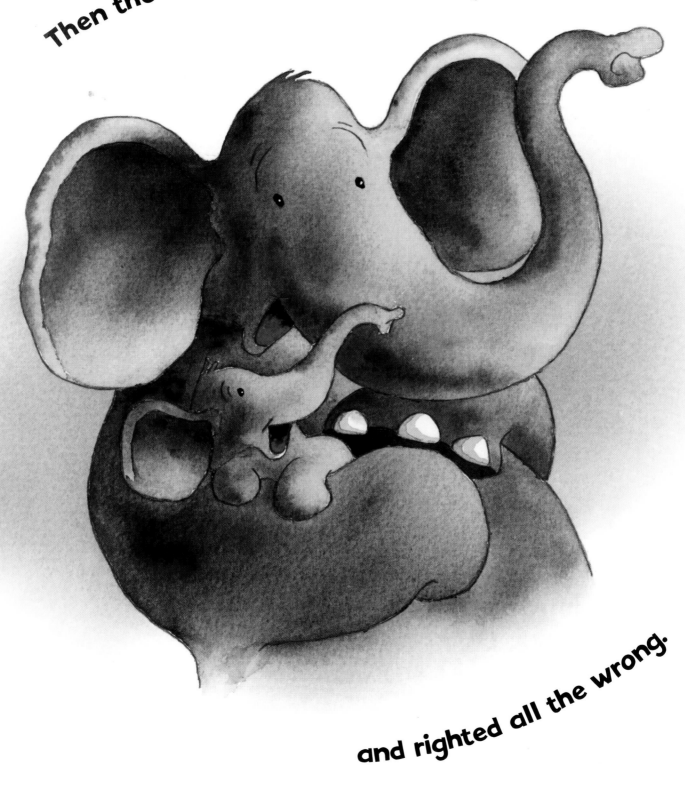

and righted all the wrong.

And now the long-lost babies
are back where they belong.

And every little creature has been comforted and fed

And cuddled by their *real* mums, who put them back to bed.

Except for two small babies who preferred their other mother . . .

So Mum kept the gorilla

and Gorilla kept my brother!